Pop-Pop Says YES

To Almost Anything

Written by J.R. Buchta

Illustrated by Daniela Frongia

Pop-Pop Says Yes: To Almost Anything

Copyright © 2024 by John Buchta

Library of Congress Control Number: 2024913634

ISBN 979-8-9869895-7-0 (Paperback)
ISBN 979-8-9869895-8-7 (Hardcover)
ISBN 979-8-9869895-9-4 (Ebook)

JUVENILE FICTION / Family / Grandparents
JUVENILE FICTION / Humorous Stories

Illustrations and cover art by Daniela Frongia at caisarts.com
Interior and cover design by Michelle M. White at mmwbooks.com

Printed in Yardley, Pennsylvania, USA by Warbucks, Inc.

For more information, visit www.warbucksbooks.com

For permissions and bulk book orders, contact emily@warbucksbooks.com

WARBUCKS

Yardley, Pennsylvania, USA

Sim Taip Tak Si
Eny
Wi Ya Eny Evet
Ya Jes Evet Ano
Òc Ano Ya
Eny Yebo Ano Jah Iva Aye Yes Awo Yebo Da Òc Ano
Jes Taip Evet Si Da Aye Ja Igen Yebo Da Jah
Jo Да Iva Iva Tak Jo Bai Yes Ja Igen Jo Да Oui Yebo Iva
Iva Po Yes Da Igen Evet Ja Si
Sim Bai Yebo Taip Iva Si Aye Da Òc Jo Да Po Bai Igen Taip Po
Sic Tak Yebo Ja Taip Ano Aye Jah Sic Oui Si Tak Jah
Òc Ja Tak Da Iva Wi Ano Yes Да Bai Evet Kyllä
Da Awo Po Kyllä Ya Jes Ano
Jes Ano Wi Si Oui Evet Wi Aye Jo
Jes Taip Sim Ja Oui Sim Taip Bai Wi
Sim Igen Iva Igen Oui Ya Да Sim
Jah En Òc Ya Jo Oui Yes Igen
Kyllä Òc Awo Jes Yebo Ya Da Bai
Awo Oui Evet Eny Sim Da Wi

Want to do something fun? Ask Pop-Pop!

He says yes to almost anything.

Want to play,
want a treat,
want to see something neat?

Pop-Pop is your man.

He's willing and able to take on anything that makes his grandchildren happy.

Wherever you go, whatever you do, it's always more fun with Pop-Pop.

Do something thrilling? . . . He's willing!

Something to eat? . . . Salty or sweet?

Somewhere to go? . . . Just let him know!

Make a list of your favorite things and do them all with Pop-Pop.

He will say yes to almost anything.

SEEK AND FIND THE HIDDEN WORD:
Find the word "YES" on every page!

Can we go to the aquarium?

Can we get a pizza?

Can we go to the movies?

Can we feed the dog?

Can we go to the zoo?

Can we go to the bakery?

Can we plant a garden?

Can we go to the beach?

Can we help wash the car?

Can we get ice cream?

Can we go to the amusement park?

Can we go to the baseball game?

Can we go to the pool?

Can we go to the firehouse?

Can we go to the lake?

Can we help rake the leaves?

Will you help us with our homework?

Can we go to the playground?

Can we go to the library?

Can we help do the laundry?

Can we read a book?

Can we build a snowman?

Can we go to the toy store?

Can we bake a cake?

Can we help take out the trash?

Can we go to the museum?

Can we have a sleepover at your house?

Pop-Pop, will you ever stop loving us?

NO!

About the Illustrator

Daniela Frongia, also known as Caisarts, is a talented international children's book illustrator with over 14 years of professional experience. Born in Sardinia, Italy, in 1979, Daniela developed a passion for drawing at the age of 5, initially focusing on Disney characters before discovering the anime world.

After graduating from Art School and gaining various art-related experiences, Daniela made the decision to relocate to London, UK. It was in London that she held her first personal art exhibition, marking a significant milestone in her artistic journey. Embracing the digital realm, Daniela found greater flexibility in her work, allowing her to pursue her love of travel. With just her Wacom Cintiq, she can create art from virtually anywhere.

About the Author

J.R. Buchta, a.k.a. Pops to Mack, Coop, and Leo, was born and raised in Philadelphia PA. As a youngster, he expressed an interest in music and spent most of his early life in the performing arts as a singer-songwriter. After graduating from the University of Pennsylvania, he entered the business world and made a career in marketing for various entrepreneurial ventures. Today, he resides in Bucks County PA with his wife.

His interest in writing took a turn towards children's books when his grandchildren were born and he recognized the power of their imaginations and their enjoyment of reading. He is the author of the award-winning book *The Wonderful Once: A Christmas Story* and *Pop-Pop Smells Funny But We Love Him Anyway*.

Other books by J.R. Buchta

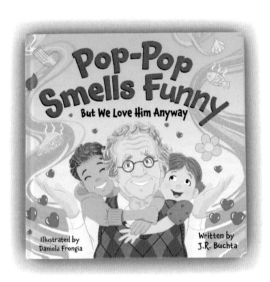

For a list of current books go to warbucksbooks.com

Made in the USA
Monee, IL
28 September 2024